Published by Darf Children's Books
An imprint of Darf Publishers Ltd
277 West End Lane
West Hampstead
London
NW6 1QS

The Tree
By Bárður Oskarsson

Originally published as *Træið*

Translated by Marita Thomsen
Edited by Beth Cox

A catalogue record of this book is available from the British Library.

Printed and bound in China by Imago

ISBN-13: 978-1-85077-327-6

www.darfpublishers.co.uk

BÁRÐUR OSKARSSON

THE TREE

darf
children's
books

...

On his way home from the shop, Bob stopped.
I wonder what is on the other side of that tree
over there, he thought.

He had been all the way over to the tree once. But before he could see what was on the other side of it a dog had come along and Bob had run away.

As Bob was thinking, Hilbert came walking towards him.

"Why are you just standing there?" Hilbert asked.

"I have never been to the other side of that tree," said Bob. "I would like to see what is there."

"Oh, there are just more trees, dogs and other animals. Nothing special really," said Hilbert.

He was about to talk about something else...

"WHAT? YOU'VE BEEN THERE?" Bob was amazed.

"Oh yes, several times. In fact, as there's nothing interesting there, I've been much further."

"Further away than the tree?" asked Bob, dropping his carrot.

He couldn't quite imagine what could be further away than the tree.

"Oh yes, I have travelled around the whole world," said Hilbert.

"AROUND THE WHOLE WORLD?"

Bob thought he had heard wrong. It sounded just a little incredible. He hesitated. Hilbert was never gone for long. It would take a long time to travel around the whole world...

"How can you have been around the world, when you are always here?" asked Bob.

"Well, you may not know this, but I can fly. So it doesn't take long."

"FLY!" shouted Bob. He nearly fell over.

It seemed totally outrageous that Hilbert could fly.

"I have never *seen* you fly," said Bob suspiciously. "How do you do it?"

"I have always been able to fly. I run and then
I just jump into the air... And then I'm flying,"
said Hilbert. "You haven't seen me, because I fly
really quickly. And I also fly very high in the sky."

Bob picked up his carrot. "Show me," he said.
He still couldn't quite believe it.

"I've been flying all morning. I'm too tired now.
I have to lie flat in the air for so long,"
said Hilbert.

"Can't you fly just a little way?" asked Bob.
"Just quickly up in the sky and down again?"

"No, not now. Maybe some other time..."

Hilbert glanced up towards the sky, over at the
tree, and then back up at the sky again.

"Fine..." said Bob.

And they stood there looking at each other.

"Right, I have to go to the shop," said Hilbert.

And he left...

Walking.

Bob looked over at the tree for a long time
before he went home.

...

...